Sky the Blue Fairy

For everyone who
believes in fairies

Special thanks to
Sue Bentley

ISBN-13: 978-0-439-74684-7
ISBN-10: 0-439-74684-1

20 19 18 17 16 15 14 13 12   11 12 13 14 15/0

Printed in the U.S.A.   40

Sky the Blue Fairy

by Daisy Meadows

illustrated by Georgie Ripper

SCHOLASTIC INC.

New York   Toronto   London   Auckland   Sydney
Mexico City   New Delhi   Hong Kong   Buenos Aires

The
Fairyland
Palace

Maze

Fores

Orchard

Black
Po

Meadow

Tower

Beach

Tidepools

Rainspell Island

Cold winds blow and thick ice forms,
I conjure up this fairy storm.
To seven corners of the human world
the Rainbow Fairies will be hurled!

I curse every part of Fairyland,
with a frosty wave of my icy hand.
For now and always, from this day,
Fairyland will be cold and gray!

Ruby, Amber, Sunny, and Fern
are safe and sound. Now Rachel
and Kirsty must track down
Sky the Blue Fairy!

Contents

A Magic Messenger

"The water's really warm!" Rachel Walker said, laughing. She was sitting on a rock, dipping her toes in one of Rainspell Island's deep blue tide pools. Her friend Kirsty Tate was looking for shells on the rocks nearby.

"Be careful not to slip, Kirsty!" called

Mrs. Tate. She was sitting farther down the beach with Rachel's mom.

"OK, Mom!" Kirsty yelled back. She looked down at her bare feet, and a patch of green seaweed beneath them began to move. There was something blue and shiny tangled up in the seaweed. "Rachel! Come over here," she shouted.

Rachel hopped across the rocks. "What is it?" she asked.

Kirsty pointed to the seaweed. "There's something blue under there," she said. "I wonder if it could it be . . ."

"Sky the Blue Fairy?" Rachel said eagerly.

A few days before, Rachel and Kirsty had discovered a magical secret. The wicked Jack Frost had banished the seven Rainbow Fairies from Fairyland with a magic spell. Now the fairies were hidden all over Rainspell Island. Until they were all found there would be no color in Fairyland. Rachel and Kirsty had promised the Fairy King and Queen that they would help find the fairies.

The seaweed twitched.

Rachel felt her heart beat faster.

"Maybe the fairy is all tangled up,"
she whispered. "Like Fern was when she
landed in the ivy on the tower."

Fern was the Green Rainbow Fairy.
Rachel and Kirsty had already found Fern
and her sisters Ruby, Amber, and Sunny.

Suddenly, a crab crawled out from under
the seaweed at Kirsty's feet.
The crab was bright
blue and very shiny.
Tiny rainbows
sparkled across its
shell. It didn't
look like any of the
other crabs on the beach.

Kirsty and Rachel smiled at each other.
This must be more of Rainspell Island's
special magic!

"Oh, no! Fairy in trouble!" the crab

muttered in a tiny voice. It sounded scratchy, like two pebbles rubbing together.

"Did you hear that?" Rachel gasped.

The crab stopped and peered up at the girls with his little stalk eyes. Then he stood up on his back legs.

"What's he doing?" Kirsty asked in surprise.

The crab pointed one claw toward some rocks farther along the beach, under the cliffs. He rushed forward a few steps, then came back and looked up at Rachel and Kirsty again. "Over there," he said.

"I think he wants us to follow him," Rachel said.

"Yes! Yes!" said the little crab, clicking

his claws. He set off sideways across a large, flat rock.

Kirsty turned to Rachel. "Maybe he knows where Sky is!"

"I hope so," Rachel replied, her eyes shining.

The crab moved off the rocks and headed across a stretch of sand. Rachel and Kirsty followed him. It was a hot, sunny day. Seagulls flew over the beach on strong, white wings.

"Rachel, Kirsty, it's almost lunchtime!" called Mrs. Walker. "We're going back to Dolphin Cottage."

Kirsty looked at Rachel in dismay. "But we have to stay here and look for the Blue Fairy!" she whispered.

The little crab jumped up and down, kicking up tiny puffs of sand. "Follow me, follow me!" he said. The girls couldn't leave him now!

Rachel thought quickly. "Mom?" she called back. "Could we have a picnic here instead, please?"

Mrs. Walker smiled. "Why not? It's a beautiful day. And we should make the most of the last three days of our vacation. I'll head back to the cottage with Kirsty's mom and make some sandwiches. You girls stay out of the water until we get back, OK?"

Only three days, thought Kirsty, *and three more Rainbow Fairies to find: Sky, Inky, and Heather!*

The two girls waved as their moms headed off toward the cottages. Kirsty turned to Rachel. "We'd better hurry. They'll be back soon."

The crab set off again, this time over a big slippery rock. Rachel and Kirsty

climbed
carefully after
him. Rachel
saw him stop next
to a small tide pool.
There were lots of pretty
pink shells in it.

"Is the fairy in one of the tide
pools?" she asked. "Is it this one?"

The crab looked
into the pool. He
scratched the top
of his head with
one claw,
looking
puzzled.
Then he
hurried
away.

"I guess not," Kirsty said.

"What about here?" Rachel said, stopping by another pool. This one had tiny silver fish swimming in it.

But the crab shook his claw at them and kept going.

"Not this one, either," said Kirsty.

Suddenly, Rachel spotted a large tide pool. It was all by itself, right at the foot

of the cliff. "Let's try that one," she said, pointing.

Kirsty ran over.

The sky was reflected in the surface of the pool like a shiny, blue mirror.

Rachel caught up with her friend. She leaned over and looked into the water.

The crab scuttled up behind them, his stalk eyes wiggling like crazy. When he dipped his claw into the pool, the water fizzed like ginger ale.

"Fairy!" cried the little crab, lifting his claw out of the water. Blue sparkles dripped off it and landed in the pool with a sizzle. The entire pool was shimmering with magic!

Bubble Trouble

"Thank you, little crab," Rachel said. She crouched down and stroked the top of the crab's shell.

The crab waved one claw at her, then dived into the water. He sank to the sandy bottom and disappeared under some seaweed.

Kirsty peered into the tide pool. "Can

you see the Blue Fairy, Rachel?" she asked.

Rachel shook her head.

Kirsty sighed, disappointed. "I can't, either."

"Do you think Jack Frost's goblins found her first?" Rachel said.

"I hope not!" Kirsty shuddered. "Those goblins will do anything to stop the Rainbow Fairies from getting back to Fairyland."

Just then, Rachel and Kirsty heard a sweet voice singing a song. "With silver bells and cockle shells, and pretty maids all in a row . . ."

"Oh!" Rachel gasped. "It's so pretty! Do you think it's the little crab?"

Kirsty shook her head. "His voice was all gritty."

"You're right," Rachel agreed. "This voice sounds tinkly — more like a fairy!"

"I think the singing is coming from that seaweed," said Kirsty, pointing into the tide pool.

Rachel peered into the water. She could see something unusual in the rippling seaweed. "Look!" she said.

Just then, a huge bubble came bobbing out of the seaweed. It floated toward the surface of the pool.

Rachel and Kirsty watched with wide eyes. There was a tiny girl inside the bubble! She waved at them and fluttered her rainbow-colored wings.

"Oh!" Kirsty gasped. "It's her! I think we've found Sky the Blue Fairy!"

The fairy pressed her hands against the curved sides of the bubble. She wore a short, sparkly dress and knee-high boots the color of bluebells. Her earrings and headband were made of little stars.

"Please help me!" Sky said. Her tiny voice sounded like bubbles popping.

Suddenly, a cold breeze swept through Rachel's hair. A dark shadow fell across the tide pool. The glowing blue water turned gray. It was as if a cloud had covered the sun.

Rachel looked up. The sun was still shining brightly overhead. "What's happening?" she cried.

Kirsty heard a strange hissing sound. She glanced around in alarm.

A layer of frost was creeping across the rocks toward them, covering the beach in a crisp, white blanket.

"Jack Frost's goblins must be very close," Kirsty said, feeling worried.

Inside her bubble, Sky shivered as ice began to cover the tide pool.

"Oh, no! She's going to be trapped,"
Kirsty cried.

Sky's bubble had stopped bobbing in
the water. Now it hung very still, frozen
into the ice. Rachel and Kirsty could see
that Sky looked very scared.

"Poor Sky! We have to rescue her!"
Rachel exclaimed. "But how can we melt
all that ice?"

"I know!" said Kirsty. "Why don't we
look in our magic bags?"

The Fairy Queen had given Rachel
and Kirsty bags with very special gifts in
them, to use for helping fairies in trouble.

"Of course!" Rachel said. Then she
frowned. "Oh, no! I left them in my
backpack. It's on the other side of the tide
pools, way down the beach!"

Goblins on Ice

"I'll run back and grab the magic bags,"
Rachel said, jumping quickly to her feet.

"OK," Kirsty said. She blew on her
hands to warm them up. The frost was
making the air very cold. "I'll stay here
with Sky. But hurry!"

"I will," Rachel promised. She scrambled

back over the rocks and onto the sandy beach.

Rachel's backpack was lying right where she'd left it. She reached inside and pulled out one of the magic bags. It was glowing with a soft golden light. When she opened it, a cloud of glitter sprayed out. Rachel slid her hand into the bag. There was something inside, smooth like a pebble. She pulled it out and looked closely at it. It was a tiny blue stone, shaped like a raindrop.

Rachel was confused. The stone was pretty, but how could it help?

Just then, the blue stone began to glow in her hand. It became warmer and warmer until it was almost too hot to hold. As it grew hotter, it glowed fiery red. Rachel curled her fingers around the raindrop stone and smiled. They could use it to melt the ice and set Sky free!

She ran back to the tide pool as fast as she could. But when she reached the rocks, she stopped dead in her tracks. Kirsty was still standing by Sky's frozen pool, but she wasn't alone anymore. Two ugly goblins were skating on the ice next to her!

"Go away!" Kirsty was shouting at the goblins, waving her hands.

Rachel could tell that Kirsty was really angry. Rachel didn't feel scared, now that she had fairy magic to help fight the goblins.

"Go away yourself!" one of the goblins yelled rudely at Kirsty. He held his arms out to his sides and slid across the ice on one foot.

Kirsty tried to grab the other goblin, but he dodged out of reach. "Can't catch me!" he cried.

"Hee, hee! The fairy can't get out of the bubble!" The other goblin laughed. His bulging eyes gleamed as he did a little twirl on the ice.

"We're going to get her out!" Kirsty told him. "We're going to find *all* the

Rainbow Fairies. And then Fairyland will get its colors back!"

"Oh no, it won't," said the goblin. He wrinkled his nose and stuck out his tongue.

"Jack Frost's magic is too strong," said the other goblin. "You girls can't do anything about it. Hey, look at me!" He pointed one foot behind himself and spun around the pool. But the ice was very slippery. He skidded sideways and crashed right into his friend.

Splat!

"Clumsy!" the other goblin snapped angrily.

"You should have moved out of the way," grumbled the clumsy one, rubbing his bottom.

Then the goblins tried to stand up. But their feet skidded in all directions and they fell over again in a heap. Rachel saw her chance. She ran to the edge of the pool and threw the magical blue stone onto the ice.

Suddenly, there was a *fizz* and a *bang*!
A shower of golden sparks shot into the
air and the ice began to melt. A big hole
appeared in the center of the pool.

"Ow! Hot! Hot!" yelled the goblins,
sliding around on the ice. They scrambled
to the edge of the pool and hurried
away, their big feet slapping on the rocks
as they ran.

"They're gone!" Kirsty said in relief.

Rachel peered into the pool. "I hope
Sky isn't hurt," she said.

All the ice had melted and the water
reflected the blue sky again. Sky's bubble
was floating just below the surface.

Rachel saw Sky sit up inside the
bubble and look around. Her eyes
were big and scared,
and she looked
very pale.

Kirsty put her hand
in the water. It was still
warm from the magic
stone. "Don't be afraid, Sky,"
she said. Very gently, Kirsty moved her
hand closer to Sky and poked her finger
into the bubble.

Pop!

Sky tumbled out of the bubble and
into the water. She swam up to the
surface, her golden hair streaming
behind her.

Kirsty leaned over and fished the fairy
out. Sky felt like a tiny wet leaf. Kirsty

placed her gently on a rock in the sun. "There you are, little fairy," she whispered.

Sky propped herself up on one elbow. Water dripped from every part of her, but there were no blue sparkles now. "Thank you for helping me," she whispered in a weak voice.

Kirsty frowned at Rachel. "Something's really wrong. All the fairies we found before had fairy dust. What happened to Sky's sparkles?"

"I don't know," said Rachel. "And she looks really pale, almost white."

It was true. Sky's dress was so pale that the girls could hardly tell it was blue at all.

Kirsty bit her lip. "It looks like Jack Frost's magic took away her color!"

Just then, the blue crab scuttled out of the

water and made his way across the rock to Sky. "Oh dear, oh dear," he muttered. "Poor little fairy."

Sky shivered and wrapped her arms around her body. "I'm so cold and sleepy," she whispered.

Kirsty felt a pang of alarm. "What's wrong, Sky? Did the goblins get too close to you?"

Sky nodded weakly. "Yes, and now I can't get warm."

"We have to help her," Rachel said.

"But how?" asked Kirsty. She looked

down at Sky in dismay. The fairy was curled up in a tiny ball with her eyes closed.

Rachel felt tears sting behind her eyelids.

Poor Sky. She looked really sick. What was going to happen to her?

Little Crab's Great Idea

Rachel spotted something moving down on the rock. "Look!" she said. The little blue crab was wiggling his front claws wildly.

"He's trying to tell us something," said Kirsty.

The girls crouched down.

"Don't worry," the crab said in his gritty voice. "My friends will help us." He scurried up to the top of the highest rock and snapped his claws in the air.

"What's he doing?" Kirsty asked. Then she stared in amazement.

Lots and lots of crabs crawled out of the tide pools around them. Big ones, little ones, all different colors. Their claws made scratchy noises on the pebbles.

The blue crab wiggled his eyes and clicked his claws, pointing up at the sky, then down at the ground. His friends scrambled away in all directions. Their little stalk eyes waved around as they poked their claws into the cracks between the rocks.

Rachel and Kirsty looked at each other, confused. "What's going on?" asked Rachel.

All of a sudden, Kirsty spotted a tiny pink crab tugging and tugging at something in the rock.

With a crunch, the crab tumbled over backward. It held a fluffy white seagull feather in its claws. The crab scrambled up again, waving the feather in the air. One by one, the other crabs searched for more feathers. Then the blue crab waved them over to to the rock where Sky lay. Very carefully, he tucked the feathers around the Blue Fairy. His friends gathered more and more feathers, until the fairy was lying in a cozy feather bed.

"They're trying to warm up Sky with seagull feathers!" Kirsty said.

Rachel held her breath. There were so many feathers now that she couldn't see the fairy at all. *Will the blue crab's idea work?* she wondered.

There was the tiniest wriggle in the feather nest. A faint puff of blue sparkles fizzed up.

POP

It smelled like blueberries. One pale blue star wobbled upward and disappeared in the air with a *pop*.

"Fairy dust!" Rachel whispered.

"But there's not very much of it," Kirsty pointed out.

There was another wriggle from inside the nest. The feathers fell apart to reveal the Blue Fairy. Her dress was still very pale. She opened her big, blue eyes and sat up.

She looked up at Rachel and Kirsty. "Hello, I'm Sky the Blue Fairy. Who are you?" she said in a sleepy voice.

"I'm Kirsty," said Kirsty.

"And I'm Rachel," said Rachel.

"Thank you for frightening the goblins away," said Sky. "And thank you, little crab, for finding all these nice, warm feathers." She tried to unfold her wings, but they were too crumpled. "My poor wings," said the fairy, her eyes filling with tiny tears.

"The feathers have helped, but Sky still can't fly," Kirsty said.

"Maybe the other Rainbow Fairies can help," Rachel said.

Sky looked up excitedly. "Do you know where my sisters are?" she asked.

"Oh, yes," said Kirsty. "So far, we've found Ruby, Amber, Sunny, and Fern."

"They are safe in the pot at the end of the rainbow," Rachel added.

"Could you take me to them, please?" said Sky. "I'm sure they will help make me better." She tried to stand up, but her legs were too wobbly and she had to sit down again.

"Here, let me carry you," Rachel offered. She cupped her hands and scooped up the feather nest with the fairy inside.

Sky waved at the little blue crab and his friends. "Good-bye. Thank you again for helping me."

"Good-bye, good-bye!" The blue crab waved his

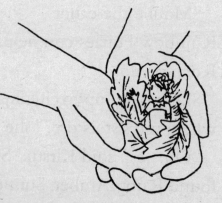

claw. His friends waved, too, their eyes shining proudly. They had never rescued a Rainbow Fairy before.

Kirsty and Rachel glanced at each other as they walked across the pebbles. Sky was being very brave, but the goblins had come closer to her than to any of the other Rainbow Fairies. And now the Blue Fairy was hardly blue at all!

Back to the Pot!

Rachel and Kirsty hurried across the
beach and into the woods. Rachel
carried Sky very carefully. The fairy lay
curled in a ball inside the warm feathers,
her cheek resting on her pale hands.

"Here's the clearing with the willow
tree," Kirsty said.

The smell of oranges hung in the air, tickling their noses. Rachel glanced around and spotted a tiny fairy. She was hovering over a patch of daisies, collecting nectar in an acorn cup.

"Look!" Rachel said. "It's Amber the Orange Fairy."

"Hello again, Rachel and Kirsty!" Amber fluttered over and settled on Rachel's shoulder.

Then Amber saw Sky lying curled up in Rachel's hand. "Sky! Oh, no! Sky, what happened? I have to call the others," she cried. She waved her wand and a fountain of sparkling orange bubbles sprayed into the air.

The other Rainbow Fairies fluttered up
all over the clearing. The air sparkled
with red, orange, yellow, and green fairy
dust. Bubbles, flowers, tiny butterflies, and
leaves sprinkled the grass.

Rachel and Kirsty watched as the
fairies gathered around Sky. The Blue
Fairy sat up slightly and gave a weak
smile, happy to see her sisters. Then she
flopped back into her nest of feathers.

"Oh, Sky!" cried Fern, the gentle Green Fairy.

"Why is she so pale?" Sunny asked.

"The goblins got really close to her," Rachel explained. "They froze the pond. Sky was trapped in a bubble under the ice."

"Ooooh! That's terrible." Sunny shuddered.

"Kirsty shouted at them and tried to catch them," Sky whispered.

"Thank you. You are so brave!" said Ruby the Red Fairy, then she flew high into the air. "We must think of something to help Sky! Oh, I know! Let's ask Bertram for his advice!"

The fairy sisters sped toward the willow tree, their wings flashing brightly in the air. Rachel and Kirsty carried Sky over in her feathery nest.

The pot at the end of the rainbow lay on its side under the willow's hanging branches. The Rainbow Fairies were living there until all seven sisters had been found and they could go back to Fairyland.

As Rachel put Sky down next to the pot, a large green frog hopped out.

"Miss Sky!" he croaked, looking pleased.

"Hello, Bertram." Sky gave another weak smile.

"The goblins came very close to Sky, and now she's really cold. We have to make her warm so she gets her color back," Fern explained.

Bertram looked very worried. "Jack Frost's goblins are so cruel," he said. "You must all stay close to the pot so that I can protect you."

"Don't worry," said Sunny, giving Sky a hug. "You'll feel better soon."

Sky nodded, but she didn't answer. Her eyes started to close. She was so pale, her arms and legs seemed almost see-through.

Rachel and Kirsty watched the rest of the Rainbow Fairies exchange worried glances. "Oh, Bertram, what if the goblins have hurt Sky forever?" asked Fern. "What can we do to save her?"

The Fairy Ring

Bertram looked very serious. "I think it's time for you fairies to try a spell."

Amber frowned. "It might not work with only four of us. Rainbow Magic needs seven fairies!"

"But Bertram's right, we have to try," Ruby said. "Maybe we can do a *small* spell. Quick, let's make a fairy ring."

The Rainbow Fairies fluttered
into a circle in the air
above Sky.

Rachel noticed a
black-and-yellow
queen bee and a
small gray squirrel
watching from the
edge of the glade.
"Queenie and
Fluffy have come
to watch the spell,"
she whispered to
Kirsty. Queenie the
bee had helped Sunny
get her wand back after
the goblins stole it. Fluffy
the squirrel had carried
Fern, Rachel, and Kirsty back to

the pot when the goblins had
been chasing them.
"Ready, sisters!" said
Ruby. She lifted her
wand. *In a fairy
ring we fly, to
bring blue color
back to Sky!"*
she chanted.
The other fairies
waved their wands.
Four different
colors of fairy dust
sparkled in the air —
red, orange, yellow, and
green. The dust covered
Sky in a glittering cloud as
she lay in the nest of feathers on
the soft green grass.

"Something's happening!" Kirsty said. Through the cloud of dust, she could see that Sky's little dress and knee-high boots were turning bluer and bluer. "The spell is working!"

Whoosh!

A shimmering cloud of blue stars shot into the air. They drifted up to the sky, where they faded away with tiny *pop*s.

"We did it!" cheered Amber, turning a cartwheel in the air, while Sunny clapped her hands in delight.

"Hooray for Rainbow Magic!" shouted Ruby.

Sky yawned and sat up. She brushed the feathers away and looked down at herself. Her face lit up. Her dress was blue again! "My wings feel strong enough to fly now," she said. She flapped them twice, then zoomed into the air. She did a twirl, and her wings flashed with rainbows. "Thank you, sisters!"

The Rainbow Fairies gathered around
Sky, hugging and kissing her. The air
around them bubbled with fairy dust —
red, orange, yellow, green, and blue. It was
almost a whole rainbow!

Rachel and Kirsty grinned.

Fern swooped down and scooped up an armful of seagull feathers. "You won't need these anymore!" She laughed, tickling Sky with a long, white one.

"But I think I might know what to do with them!" said Sky. She flew down to the edge of the pot and peeked in. "It's so cozy!" she said, admiring the tiny chairs and tables made of twigs and the giant shell bed. Then Sky fluttered over to the rest of the feathers and gathered them up. "I thought we could put these on our bed. They'll be very warm and soft."

Her fairy sisters looked delighted. "Thanks, Sky. What a good idea!" said Ruby.

"Let's have a welcome-home feast," said Fern. "With wild strawberries and clover juice."

Amber did another cartwheel.

"Hooray! Rachel and Kirsty, you're invited, too!"

"Thank you, but we have to go." Rachel looked at her watch. "Our moms will be waiting at the beach with our picnic."

"Oh, that's right!" Kirsty remembered, jumping up. She felt a little disappointed that she wouldn't have a chance to taste some fairy food. But she also didn't want her mom to be worried. "Good-bye! We'll be back again soon!"

The fairies sat on the edge of the pot
and waved to the girls. Queenie, Fluffy,
and Bertram the Frog waved, too.
"Good-bye! Good-bye!"

Sky fluttered in the air next to Rachel and Kirsty as they walked back across the clearing. Tiny rainbows sparkled on her wings. Her dress and boots glowed bright blue, and a blueberry smell filled the air.

"Thank you so much, Rachel and Kirsty," she said. "Now five Rainbow Fairies are safe."

"We'll find Inky and Heather, too," Kirsty said. "I promise."

"Yes," Rachel agreed.

As they made their way back to the
beach, Rachel looked at Kirsty. "Do you
think we can find them in time? We only
have two days of vacation left. And the
goblins are getting much closer. They
almost caught Sky today!"

Kirsty squeezed her friend's hand and
smiled. "Don't worry. Nothing is going to
stop us from keeping our promise to the
Rainbow Fairies!"

RAINBOW magic™

THE RAINBOW FAIRIES

Ruby, Amber, Sunny, Fern,
and Sky are all safe.
But where is

Inky the Indigo Fairy?

Time is running out!
Join Kirsty and Rachel's adventure
in this special sneak peek. . . .

A Fairy-tale Beginning

"Rain, rain, go away." Rachel Walker sighed. "Come again another day!"

She and her friend Kirsty Tate stared out of the attic window. Raindrops splashed against the glass, and the sky was full of purplish-black clouds.

"Isn't it a horrible day?" Kirsty said. "But it's nice and cozy in here, at least."

She looked around Rachel's small attic bedroom. There was just enough room for a brass bed with a patchwork quilt, a comfy armchair, and an old bookcase.

"You know what the weather on Rainspell is like," Rachel pointed out. "It changes all the time. It might be hot and sunny very soon!"

Both girls had come to Rainspell Island for a week-long vacation. The Walkers were staying in Mermaid Cottage, while the Tates were in Dolphin Cottage next door.

Kirsty frowned. "Yes, but what about Inky the Indigo Fairy?" she asked. "We have to find her today."

Rachel and Kirsty shared a wonderful secret. They were trying to find the seven Rainbow Fairies. The fairies brought color to Fairyland, but mean Jack Frost had sent them away with a wicked spell. Fairyland would be cold and gray until all seven fairies had been found again.

Rachel thought about Ruby, Amber, Sunny, Fern, and Sky, who were all safe now in the pot at the end of the rainbow. Rachel and Kirsty only had Inky the Indigo Fairy and Heather the Violet Fairy left to find. But how could they look for the fairies while they were stuck indoors?

"Remember what the Fairy Queen said?" Rachel reminded Kirsty.

Kirsty nodded. "She said the magic would come to us." Suddenly, she looked scared. "Maybe the rain is Jack Frost's magic. Maybe he's trying to stop us from finding Inky."

"Oh, no!" Rachel said. "Let's hope it

stops soon. But what will we do while we're waiting?"

Kirsty thought for a minute. Then she went over to the bookcase. It was filled with dusty, old books, and she pulled one out. It was so big, she had to use two hands to hold it.

"*The Big Book of Fairy Tales,*" Rachel read out, looking at the cover.

"If we can't find fairies, at least we can read about them!" Kirsty grinned.

The two girls sat down on the bed and put the book on their knees. Kirsty was about to turn the first page when Rachel gasped. "Kirsty, look at the cover! It's purple. A really deep purplish-blue."

"That's indigo," Kirsty whispered. "Oh, Rachel! Do you think Inky could be trapped inside?"

"Let's see," Rachel said. "Hurry up, Kirsty. Open the book!"

But Kirsty had spotted something else. "Rachel," she said shakily. "It's *glowing*."

Rachel looked. Kirsty was right. Some pages in the middle of the book were gleaming with a soft purplish-blue light.

Kirsty opened the book. The ink on the pages was glowing indigo. For a moment, Kirsty thought that Inky might fly out of the pages, but there was no sign of her. On the first page was a picture of a wooden soldier. Above the picture were the words: *The Nutcracker*.

"Oh!" Rachel said. "I know this story. I went to see the ballet at Christmas."

"What's it about?" Kirsty asked.

"Well, a girl named Clara gets a wooden nutcracker soldier for Christmas," Rachel explained. "He comes to life and takes her to the Land of Sweets." They looked down at a brightly colored picture of a Christmas tree. A little girl was asleep beside it, holding a wooden soldier.

On the next page there was a picture of snowflakes whirling and swirling through a dark forest. "Aren't the pictures great?" Kirsty said. "The snow looks so real."

Rachel frowned. For a moment, she had thought the snowflakes were moving. Gently she put out her hand and touched the page. It felt cold and wet!

"Kirsty," she whispered. "It *is* real!" She held out her hand. There were white snowflakes on her fingers.

Kirsty looked down at the book again, her eyes wide. The snowflakes started to swirl from the book's pages, right into the bedroom, slowly at first, then faster and faster.

Read the rest of

THE RAINBOW FAIRIES

Inky the Indigo Fairy

to find out if the swirling snowstorm is truly magical.

RAINBOW magic™

There's Magic in Every Series!

The Rainbow Fairies

The Weather Fairies

The Jewel Fairies

The Pet Fairies

The Fun Day Fairies

The Petal Fairies

The Dance Fairies

The Music Fairies

The Sports Fairies

The Party Fairies

Read them all!

■ SCHOLASTIC

www.scholastic.com

rainbowmagiconline.com

HIT entertain

RM